CLASSICS Illustrated

George Eliot
SILAS MARNER

essay by
Andrew J. Hoffman, Ph.D
Brown University

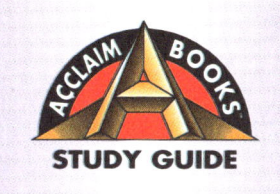

ACCLAIM BOOKS
STUDY GUIDE

CLASSICS Illustrated

Silas Marner
Originally published as Classics Illustrated no. 55

Art by Arnold Hicks
Adaption by H. Miller
Cover by Scott Hampton

For Classics Illustrated Study Guides
computer recoloring byVanHook Studios
editor: Madeleine Robins
assistant editor: Valerie D'Orazio
design: Joseph Caponsacco

Classics Illustrated: Silas Marner © Twin Circle Publishing Co.,
a division of Frawley Enterprises; licensed to First Classics, Inc.
All new material and compilation © 1997 by Acclaim Books, Inc.

Dale-Chall R.L.: 7.25

ISBN 1-57840-050-3

Classics Illustrated® is a registered trademark of the Frawley Corporation.

Acclaim Books, New York, NY
Printed in the United States

SILAS MARNER

BY GEORGE ELIOT

In the early years of the eighteenth century, Silas Marner worked at his vocation as a linen weaver in a stone cottage in the town of Raveloe, England. He had neither friends nor family and was generally feared and despised by all the townspeople: feared because of an affliction which caused him to be subject to occasional cataleptic fits, and despised because of his miserliness.

Silas Marner was a respected young man, plying his trade as a linen weaver in a secluded town known as Lantern Yard...

It was Marner's custom to escort his fiancée, Sarah, to church every Sunday...

"Look, Silas, there's William Dane! Shall we ask him to join us?"

"As my closest friend, William is always welcome to share our presence!"

"Well, if it isn't my two little love birds!"

"Hello, William! Won't you join us at the services?"

Dane accepted the invitation and joins the couple at the prayer meeting...

"You look lovelier every time I see you, Sarah!"

Suddenly...

"Something has happened to Silas! Call a doctor!"

"He'll be all right! It's just one of his cataleptic* fits! I fear Silas is hiding some accursed thing within his soul!"

*Nervous attack affecting the muscles

Panel 1: IT WAS DUE TO THESE VISITATIONS AND DANE'S DISPARAGING REMARKS, THAT SARAH GRADUALLY DEVELOPED A FORBIDDING COOLNESS TOWARDS SILAS, AND A WARMING FRIENDSHIP GREW UP BETWEEN HER AND WILLIAM DANE...

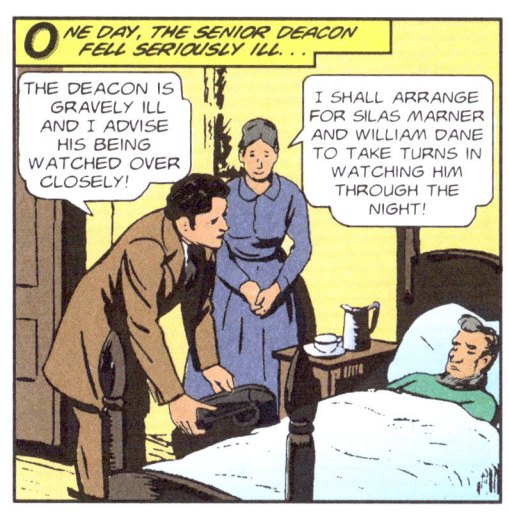

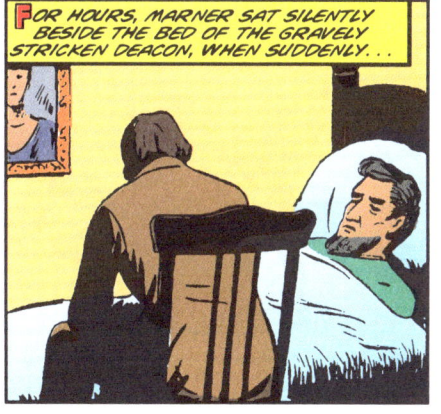

Panel 2: ONE DAY, THE SENIOR DEACON FELL SERIOUSLY ILL...
"THE DEACON IS GRAVELY ILL AND I ADVISE HIS BEING WATCHED OVER CLOSELY!"
"I SHALL ARRANGE FOR SILAS MARNER AND WILLIAM DANE TO TAKE TURNS IN WATCHING HIM THROUGH THE NIGHT!"

Panel 3: THAT NIGHT...
"HOW IS THE DEACON?"
"HIS CONDITION IS GRAVE, MASTER MARNER, AND HE BEARS CLOSE WATCHING! DANE WILL BE HERE TO RELIEVE YOU AT TWO O'CLOCK."

Panel 4: FOR HOURS, MARNER SAT SILENTLY BESIDE THE BED OF THE GRAVELY STRICKEN DEACON, WHEN SUDDENLY...

Panel 5: MARNER STIFFENED IN HIS CHAIR, HIS EYES STARING VACANTLY INTO SPACE...

Panel 6: SEVERAL HOURS LATER...
"GOOD HEAVENS! IT'S FOUR O'CLOCK! I MUST HAVE FALLEN ASLEEP!"

HE'S DEAD!
THE MINISTER, WITH SOME FRIENDS, ARRIVED IN ANSWER TO MARNER'S SUMMONS. . .
I MUST HAVE SLEPT AT LEAST FOUR HOURS; WHEN I AWOKE, HE WAS BEYOND HELP!
GO TO YOUR HOME, SILAS! I SHALL BE OVER TO SEE YOU PRESENTLY!
I JUST CANNOT UNDERSTAND WHY WILLIAM DANE DID NOT COME TO RELIEVE ME AS HE HAD PROMISED!
LATER, MARNER RECEIVED TWO VISITORS. . .
WHY, WILLIAM! WHERE. . .
SILAS, WE HAVE COME TO ESCORT YOU TO LANTERN YARD TO MEET THE CHURCH MEMBERS!
THE CHURCH MEMBERS! BUT WHY?
YOU WILL HEAR!

IN THE CHURCH VESTRY. . .
DOES THIS POCKET KNIFE BELONG TO YOU, SILAS MARNER?
WHY, YES, IT'S MINE! BUT WHAT IS THE MEANING OF THIS INTERROGATION?
THIS KNIFE WAS FOUND IN THE BUREAU BY THE DEACON'S BEDSIDE. . . IN THE VERY SPOT WHERE A BAG CONTAINING THE CHURCH'S MONEY WAS STOLEN!
BUT SURELY, YOU DON'T BELIEVE THAT I HAD ANYTHING TO DO WITH IT!
THE PROOF IS HEAVY AGAINST YOU, BROTHER MARNER! WILLIAM DANE DECLARES HE WAS UNABLE TO RELIEVE YOU BECAUSE OF SUDDEN ILLNESS; AND MOREOVER, YOU NEGLECTED THE DEAD BODY!
AS GOD IS MY WITNESS, I HAD NOTHING TO DO WITH THE THEFT OF THAT MONEY! I PLEAD WITH YOU TO BELIEVE ME! SEARCH MY HOUSE! YOU WILL FIND NOTHING THERE BUT THREE POUND FIVE OF MY OWN SAVINGS!

IN MARNER'S HOUSE, THEY TOOK UP THE SEARCH FOR THE MISSING CHURCH MONEY...

LOOK! THE BAG OF MONEY HIDDEN BEHIND THIS CHEST OF DRAWERS!

BUT, WILLIAM, YOU CAN'T POSSIBLY BELIEVE I HAD ANYTHING TO DO WITH HIDING THAT MONEY!

BROTHER MARNER, YOU WILL APPEAR AT A MEETING OF THE CHURCH MEMBERS IN THE MORNING, AND THEY WILL DRAW LOTS TO PASS ON YOUR GUILT OR INNOCENCE!

I AM SORE STRICKEN! I KNOW NOTHING! GOD WILL CLEAR ME!

SURELY, WILLIAM, YOU WILL TESTIFY THAT IN THE NINE LONG YEARS YOU HAVE KNOWN ME, I HAVE NEVER TOLD A LIE!

NEXT MORNING...

YOU HAVE HEARD THE CASE OF THE CHURCH AGAINST SILAS MARNER! THE MEMBERS WILL NOW DRAW LOTS TO DECIDE THE FATE OF THE ACCUSED!

THE LOTS WERE DRAWN...

BY YOUR LOTS, YOU HAVE FOUND SILAS MARNER GUILTY OF STEALING THE FUNDS AND BETRAYING THE CHURCH!

YOU WERE THE LAST TO SEE MY KNIFE, WILLIAM! YOU STOLE THE MONEY AND WOVE A PLOT TO LAY THE SIN AT MY DOOR! YOU MAY PROSPER FOR ALL THAT, BUT THERE IS NO JUST GOD THAT GOVERNS THE EARTH RIGHTEOUSLY, BUT A GOD OF LIES AGAINST THE INNOCENT!

THERE WAS A GENERAL SHUDDER AT THIS BLASPHEMY AND DANE ROSE MEEKLY TO HIS FEET...

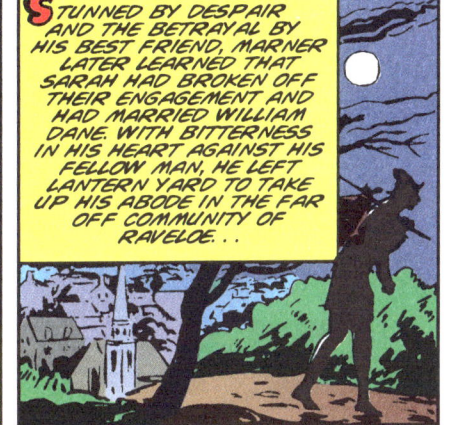

I LEAVE MY BRETHREN TO JUDGE WHETHER THIS IS THE VOICE OF SATAN OR NOT! I CAN DO NOTHING BUT PRAY FOR YOU, SILAS.

AS PUNISHMENT FOR THE CRIME OF WHICH HE WAS FOUND GUILTY, MARNER WAS SUSPENDED FROM CHURCH MEMBERSHIP UNTIL SUCH TIME AS HE WOULD CONFESS, AS A SIGN OF REPENTANCE.

STUNNED BY DESPAIR AND THE BETRAYAL BY HIS BEST FRIEND, MARNER LATER LEARNED THAT SARAH HAD BROKEN OFF THEIR ENGAGEMENT AND HAD MARRIED WILLIAM DANE. WITH BITTERNESS IN HIS HEART AGAINST HIS FELLOW MAN, HE LEFT LANTERN YARD TO TAKE UP HIS ABODE IN THE FAR OFF COMMUNITY OF RAVELOE...

IN THE FIFTEEN YEARS SINCE MARNER HAD ABANDONED LANTERN YARD FOR HIS LONELY REFUGE IN RAVELOE, HE HAD ACCUMULATED A FORTUNE AT THE TRADE OF WEAVING. . .
HEH! HEH! TWO HUNDRED AND FIFTY POUNDS IN GLISTENING GOLDEN GUINEAS. THE SOUND OF THEIR CLINKING IS MUSIC TO AN OLD MAN'S EARS!
I MUST FIND A HIDING PLACE FOR MY TREASURE BEFORE SOME SNOOPING WRETCH RELIEVES ME OF IT WHILE I'M AWAY!
PLACING THE MONEY IN A BAG, MARNER DECIDED TO HIDE IT UNDER THE FLOOR, NEAR HIS LOOM. . .
THIS SHOULD BE A SAFE PLACE FROM THE PRYING EYES OF MY NEIGHBORS, WHO, TO SAY THE LEAST, BEAR ME NO GOOD WILL.
NOW, I WILL TAKE THIS LINEN TO MRS. OSGOOD AND RECEIVE ANOTHER GOLDEN GUINEA FOR MY TREASURED COLLECTION!

ABOUT CHRISTMAS OF THE SAME YEAR, A SECOND GREAT CHANGE CAME OVER MARNER'S LIFE AND HIS HISTORY BECAME INVOLVED IN A SINGULAR MANNER WITH THE LIFE OF HIS NEIGHBORS...
IN A LARGE HOUSE KNOWN BY THE VILLAGERS AS RED HOUSE, DWELT THE WIDOWER, SQUIRE CASS, WITH HIS FOUR SONS...
GODFREY, THE ELDEST, WAS PACING THE FLOOR, AWAITING THE APPEARANCE OF HIS WORTHLESS BROTHER, DUNSTAN...
HANG THAT NO GOOD BROTHER OF MINE! WHY DOES HE KEEP ME WAITING WHEN I SEND FOR HIM?
YOU'RE MY ELDER AND BETTER, GODFREY! I WAS OBLIGED TO COME WHEN YOU SENT FOR ME!
NEVER MIND THE SARCASM, DUNSTAN. JUST SHAKE YOURSELF SOBER AND LISTEN!
IT'S ABOUT THAT MONEY I COLLECTED FOR THE SQUIRE AND GAVE TO YOU! THE SQUIRE'S SHORT OF CASH AND WILL STAND FOR NO NONSENSE! I WANT YOU TO GET THAT MONEY AND GET IT QUICKLY!

SUPPOSE, NOW, YOU GET THE MONEY YOURSELF AND SAVE ME THE TROUBLE! IT WAS YOUR BROTHERLY LOVE, YOU KNOW, THAT MADE YOU LEND IT TO ME!
PLEASE DON'T COME NEAR ME WITH THAT LOOK, ELSE I'LL KNOCK YOU DOWN!
OH, NO YOU WON'T! NOT WHILE YOU KNOW I CARRY THE SECRET OF YOUR MARRIAGE TO THAT NICE YOUNG WOMAN, MOLLY FARRAN!
YOU WOULDN'T DARE TELL THE SQUIRE! WHY, I'D. . .
CALM YOURSELF, MASTER GODFREY, AND I'LL MAKE YOU A PROPOSITION THAT WILL KEEP YOU IN THE GOOD GRACES OF THE SQUIRE, NOT TO MENTION MISS NANCY LAMMETER!
KEEP MISS NANCY'S NAME OUT OF THIS, YOU FOOL! WHAT IS THIS PROPOSITION?
WHY SIMPLY THIS. . .

LET ME TAKE WILDFIRE TO THE HUNT AND SELL HIM FOR YOU TO THE HIGHEST BIDDER! I DARE SAY HE'LL BRING AT LEAST A HUNDRED TWENTY POUNDS!

RELUCTANTLY, BUT DESPERATE FOR THE MONEY, GODFREY LET DUNSTAN TAKE WILDFIRE TO THE HUNT...

MIND YOU, KEEP SOBER, ELSE YOU'LL GET PITCHED ON YOUR HEAD!

IT'S WILDFIRE YOU'RE THINKING ABOUT, BROTHER, NOT MY HEAD! YOU'VE NEVER KNOWN ME TO SEE DOUBLE WHILE DRIVING A BARGAIN!

I NEVER THOUGHT I'D SEE THE DAY I SHOULD HAVE TO PART WITH MY FAVORITE STEED! THE BLACKMAILING SCOUNDREL!

DUNSTAN ARRIVES AT THE HUNT...

HEY-DAY, DUNSEY! I SEE YOU'RE ON YOUR BROTHER'S HORSE TODAY!

OH, I'VE SWAPPED WITH HIM! WILDFIRE'S MINE NOW!

HE'S A MIGHTY FINE ANIMAL! I WAS OFFERED A HUNDRED FIFTY THE OTHER DAY FROM A MAN OVER AT FLITTON!

I WON'T GIVE YOU A PENNY OVER ONE TWENTY-- THAT IS FINAL!

THE BARGAIN WAS SEALED...

DRIVE WILDFIRE OVER TO THE BATHERLEY STABLES AND COLLECT YOUR MONEY! BUT MIND, GET HIM THERE SAFE AND SOUND, OR THE DEAL'S OFF!

DUNSTAN LINGERED A WHILE TO WATCH THE HUNT...

WHAT A SPLENDID DAY FOR THE HUNT!

INTRIGUED BY THE PROSPECT OF WINNING THE CHASE WITH WILDFIRE, DUNSTAN WAS SEIZED WITH AN URGE TO JOIN THE HUNT BEFORE HE TURNED THE HORSE IN...
I'VE ALWAYS WANTED TO RIDE WILDFIRE IN THE HUNT, AND THIS IS AS GOOD A TIME AS ANY!
YOU'VE GOT A FINE MOUNT THERE DUNSTAN!
HE IS INDEED! I'LL WAGER HE SHOWS THE FIELD HIS DUST BEFORE THE CHASE IS OVER!
DUNSTAN, BECAUSE OF POOR HANDLING OF HIS MOUNT, FELL BEHIND...
COME ON, WILDFIRE!
THEY APPROACHED A STAKED BARRIER* IN THEIR PATH...
*SERIES OF SHARP-POINTED WOODEN POSTS.

WE MUST TAKE THIS FENCE!
SUDDENLY...
DRAT THE LUCK! I HOPE HE HASN'T BROKEN A LEG!
GREAT SCOTT! HE'S BEEN STAKED!*
*KILLED BY A SHARP-POINTED WOODEN POST
NOW I'LL HAVE TO RETURN TO RED HOUSE WITHOUT THE HORSE OR THE MONEY! THIS IS A FINE MESS I'VE COOKED UP FOR MYSELF!

IN A HEAVY MIST, AND CARRYING GODFREY'S WHIP, DUNSTAN SET OUT FOR RAVELOE...
HANG IT ALL! IN THIS HEAVY MIST, I'LL NEVER FIND THE ROAD!
DUNSTAN SAW A LIGHT SHINING THROUGH THE MURKY GLOOM...
I MUST BE NEAR THE STONE-PITS AND THAT LIGHT IS FROM MARNER'S COTTAGE!
THAT OLD MISER'S GOT MORE MONEY THAN HE'LL EVER HAVE NEED FOR! WHY NOT ASK HIM FOR A LOAN AND PROMISE HIM A GOOD RATE OF INTEREST?
WHY DIDN'T I THINK OF THIS BEFORE? IT'LL STRAIGHTEN ME OUT WITH GODFREY AND GIVE ME A FEW GUINEAS FOR MYSELF TO BOOT!

RECEIVING NO RESPONSE TO HIS KNOCKS ON THE DOOR, DUNSTAN ENTERED THE COTTAGE AND STARTED BROWSING ABOUT. NOTICING THAT THE BRICKS BY THE LOOM HAD BEEN DISTURBED, DUNSTAN PRIED AWAY...
FINALLY...
MARNER'S GOLD! I MUST GET AWAY BEFORE THE OLD SKIN-FLINT RETURNS!
HE'LL NEVER BE ABLE TO TRACK ME DOWN IN THE RAIN!
AS DUNSTAN DISAPPEARED INTO THE DARK, A STOOPED FIGURE CAME PLODDING TOWARDS THE HOUSE...
THAT FIRE NEVER LOOKED MORE INVITING! BRR! I'M SOAKED CLEAR THROUGH TO THE SKIN!
MY TREASURE!

"IT'S GONE! MY LIFE'S SAVINGS ARE GONE!"

HOPING AGAINST HOPE THAT HE HAD HIMSELF, BY SOME CHANCE, HIDDEN THE MONEY ELSEWHERE, MARNER MADE A FRANTIC SEARCH OF EVERY CORNER IN THE ROOM...

THE TRUTH FINALLY DAWNED UPON THE LUCKLESS WEAVER...

"WOE IS ME! I AM RUINED! THE MONEY I SLAVED FOR, FOR FIFTEEN YEARS, HAS BEEN STOLEN BY SOME MISERABLE WRETCH!"

IN HIS MISERY, MARNER RECALLED THAT JEM RODNEY, WHO WAS A KNOWN POACHER, HAD ONCE MADE A CALL ON HIM AND HAD SPOKEN JESTINGLY OF HIS MONEY...

"JEM RODNEY IS THE THIEF! I'LL GO TO THE RAINBOW AND MAKE HIM RESTORE HIS ILL-GOTTEN HOARD!"

UNMINDFUL OF THE ELEMENTS, MARNER HEADED STRAIGHT FOR "THE RAINBOW," THE VILLAGE TAVERN...

THE QUIET AT THE RAINBOW WAS SUDDENLY DISTURBED BY A PALE, THIN, DRENCHED FIGURE AT THE DOOR...
MASTER MARNER! WHAT'S YOUR BUSINESS HERE?
ROBBED! I'VE BEEN ROBBED! I WANT THE CONSTABLE AND THE JUSTICE, AND SQUIRE CASS, AND MR. CRACKENTHORP.
LAY HOLD ON HIM, JEM RODNEY! HE'S OFF HIS HEAD!
LAY HOLD ON HIM YOURSELF, MR. SNELL! HE'S BEEN ROBBED AND MURDERED FOR WHAT I KNOW!
RODNEY!
AY, MASTER MARNER! WHAT DO YOU WANT WITH ME?
YOU STOLE MY MONEY! GIVE IT BACK AND I WON'T SET THE CONSTABLE ON YOU! PRAY, RODNEY, GIVE IT BACK AND I'LL LET YOU HAVE A GUINEA!

ME STEAL YOUR MONEY? I'LL PITCH THIS CAN AT YOUR EYE IF YOU TALK ABOUT ME STEALING YOUR MONEY!
MR. SNELL ESTABLISHED AN ALIBI FOR JEM RODNEY. APOLOGIZING TO RODNEY, MARNER TOLD HIS STORY TO THE ASSEMBLED VILLAGERS. . .
THE VILLAGE FARRIER* TOOK IT UPON HIMSELF TO QUESTION MARNER. . .
HOW MUCH MONEY MIGHT THERE BE IN THE BAG, MASTER MARNER?
*BLACKSMITH
TWO HUNDRED SEVENTY TWO POUNDS TWELVE AND SIXPENCE*! I COUNTED IT LAST NIGHT!
*APPROXIMATELY $1,090.46
I SHALL GO WITH YOU TO EXAMINE YOUR PREMISES AND THEN REPORT YOUR LOSS TO THE CONSTABLE!
UNCONSOLED AND HEARTBROKEN, MARNER LEFT THE RAINBOW WITH THE FARRIER. . .

Next morning, concerned at Dunstan's absence...

"I'LL RIDE OVER TO BATHERLEY STABLES! DUNSTAN'S PROBABLY GONE ON A DRUNKEN SPREE AND SPENT THE NIGHT THERE!"

"THAT MUST BE THAT WORTHLESS BROTHER OF MINE, NOW!"

"WELL, MR. GODFREY, THAT'S A LUCKY BROTHER OF YOURS, THAT MASTER DUNSEY!"

"HOW DO YOU MEAN?"

"WHY, HASN'T HE BEEN HOME YET?"

"NO! WHAT HAS HAPPENED?"

Bryce told Godfrey of his brother's mishap at the hunt...

"I HOPE I'LL HAVE BETTER NEWS ANOTHER TIME!"

"HEAVEN KNOWS IT COULDN'T BE WORSE!"

Tormented by the complications that had beset his tortured life, Godfrey determined to make a clean avowal to his father the next morning. The Squire was very angry and suggested that the only way for Godfrey to straighten out his life would be to marry. He offered to intercede in Godfrey's behalf with Nancy Lammeter but Godfrey begged for time to handle the matter in his own way.

ON NEW YEAR'S EVE, A BRILLIANT CELEBRATION WAS HELD AT RED HOUSE. . .
MR. LAMMETER AND HIS DAUGHTER HAVE JUST ARRIVED, MASTER GODFREY!
I'LL GO AND FETCH THEM!
GODFREY WELCOMED MR. LAMMETER TO RED HOUSE. . .
HAVE YOU NO WORD OF GREETING FOR ME GODFREY?
YOU KNOW I'M GLAD TO SEE YOU NANCY!
INDEED! I MUST SAY YOUR ACTIONS SOMETIMES BELIE YOUR WORDS!
WHAT A HANDSOME COUPLE MASTER GODFREY AND NANCY MAKE!
WHILE GODFREY CASS WAS TAKING DRAUGHTS OF FORGETFULNESS FROM THE SWEET PRESENCE OF NANCY, A DRAMA OF A DIFFERENT SORT WAS BEING UNFOLDED IN A SMALL COTTAGE ON THE OUTSKIRTS OF RAVELOE, WHERE MOLLY FARRAN, THE SECRET WIFE OF GODFREY CASS, AND HER CHILD MADE THEIR HOME. . .

IN A DISMAL COTTAGE WHICH TO MOLLY FARRAN WAS HOME...
BYE, BYE, MOMMY?
YES, MY DEAR! WE'RE GOING ON A VISIT WE SHOULD HAVE MADE A LONG TIME AGO!
WE MUST LOOK PRETTY, BABY, FOR YOUR GRANDFATHER'S A SQUIRE, QUITE THE RICHEST MAN IN RAVELOE!
AND YOUR NO-GOOD FATHER MUST BE MADE TO TAKE CARE OF HIS CHILD IN THE MANNER BEFITTING A SQUIRE'S GRANDDAUGHTER!
STRUGGLING ALONG IN THE HEAVY STORM, MOLLY WAS DETERMINED TO LAY HER CASE BEFORE THE SQUIRE, COME WHAT MAY...
CARRYING THE CHILD IN HER ARMS, MOLLY SET OUT FOR RED HOUSE...

CLUTCHING HER CHILD, MOLLY STRUGGLED IN A RAGING BLIZZARD...
SHE WAS SOON OVERCOME WITH A LONGING TO LIE DOWN AND SLEEP...
THE CHILD, SENSING THAT SOMETHING WAS AMISS, LOOKED ABOUT FOR HELP...
MOMMY!
SUDDENLY, THE CHILD'S EYES WERE CAUGHT BY A BRIGHT LIGHT IN THE SNOW...
SHE FOLLOWED THE GLEAM...
SILAS MARNER, TRANSFIXED IN A TRANCE, WAS UNAWARE THAT THE CHILD WAS APPROACHING HIS DOOR...

STUMBLING THROUGH THE SNOW, THE CHILD ENTERED THE COTTAGE...
PITTY FIRE.
MARNER RECOVERED FROM HIS TRANCE...
I MUST HAVE BEEN STANDING HERE LONGER THAN I THOUGHT! BRRR! I'M CHILLED TO THE BONE.
ATTRACTED BY THE BLAZING HEARTH, SHE FELL ASLEEP ON MARNER'S SACK, DRYING ON THE BRICKS...
GUESS I'LL THROW A LOG ON THE FIRE!
SUDDENLY, HIS EYE CAUGHT SIGHT OF A GOLDEN MASS ON THE SACK...
GOLD! MY PRECIOUS GOLD!

STRETCHING HIS HAND FORWARD TO GRASP THE GOLDEN MASS, HIS HAND TOUCHED THE SOFT WARM CURLS...
BLESS ME, IF IT ISN'T A BABY GIRL!
THIS CANNOT BE! WHERE DID SHE COME FROM AND HOW IS IT I DID NOT SEE HER ENTER THE HOUSE?
SOME UNSEEN POWER HAS CHOSEN THIS WAY OF REPAYING ME FOR MY LOSS!
A MOMENT LATER...
WHERE MOMMY?
A DEEP ATTACHMENT FOR THE CHILD SURGED UP WITHIN THE WEAVER'S BREAST...
WE'LL FIND YOUR MOMMY BUT FIRST, UNCLE SILAS WILL FIX YOU UP WITH A BIT OF PORRIDGE.

LATER...
NOW THAT WE'VE GOT SOME FOOD INTO YOUR LITTLE TUMMY. WE'LL GO AND LOOK FOR YOUR MOMMY!
I'LL FOLLOW HER FOOT-PRINTS IN THE SNOW!
GOOD GRIEF!
POOR WOMAN! SHE'S FROZEN STIFF!
PERHAPS IT'S NOT TOO LATE TO FIND HELP FOR YOUR MOMMY, PRECIOUS!
MARNER HURRIED TO RED HOUSE TO FIND HELP FOR THE STRICKEN WOMAN...

BACK AT RED HOUSE, GODFREY'S EYES WERE RIVITED ON NANCY, SEATED NEXT TO THE SQUIRE...
SUDDENLY, HE WAS AWARE OF ALL EYES BEING FIXED ON THE DOOR...
IT'S SILAS MARNER!
MY BABY!
WHAT'S THIS! WHAT DO YOU MEAN BY COMING IN HERE THIS WAY?
I'VE COME FOR THE DOCTOR! I WANT THE DOCTOR!

WHY, WHAT'S THE MATTER, MARNER? THE DOCTOR IS HERE, BUT SAY QUIETLY WHAT YOU WANT HIM FOR.
IT'S A WOMAN! SHE'S DEAD, I THINK! IN THE SNOW AT THE STONE-PITS--NOT FAR FROM MY DOOR!
IT'S MOLLY! SHE'S DEAD!
WHAT CHILD IS IT, GODFREY?
I-I DON'T KNOW! SOME POOR WOMAN'S--SHE WAS FOUND IN THE SNOW!
YOU'D BETTER LEAVE THE CHILD HERE, MASTER MARNER!
NO, NO--I CAN'T PART WITH IT! IT CAME TO ME--I'VE A RIGHT TO KEEP IT!
DID YOU EVER HEAR THE LIKE?

GODFREY FOLLOWED DR. KIMBLE AND MARNER TO THE STONE-PITS...
AT THE STONE-PITS, MOLLY FARRAN WAS CARRIED INTO MARNER'S HOUSE, WHILE OUTSIDE, GODFREY PACED UP AND DOWN, PONDERING ON THE UNEXPECTED TURN OF EVENTS...
IF SHE'S DEAD I MAY MARRY NANCY--AND THE FUTURE SHALL HOLD NO TERRORS FOR ME--AND THE CHILD--SHE'LL BE TAKEN CARE OF!
THERE'S NOTHING TO BE DONE! SHE'S DEAD--HAS BEEN FOR HOURS I SHOULD SAY!
WHAT SORT OF WOMAN IS SHE?
A YOUNG WOMAN, BUT EMACIATED--QUITE IN RAGS! SHE'S GOT A WEDDING RING ON, HOWEVER. COME ON GODFREY, THERE'S NOTHING WE CAN DO!
I'LL OVERTAKE YOU IN A MINUTE OR TWO! I WANT TO SPEAK TO MARNER!

GODFREY ENTERED THE COTTAGE WITH A STRANGE MIXTURE OF JOY--THAT THE CHILD DID NOT RECOGNIZE HIM--AND REGRET--THAT HE COULDN'T CLAIM HER AS HIS OWN...
YOU'LL TAKE THE CHILD TO THE PARISH TOMORROW?
WHO SAYS SO? WILL THEY MAKE ME TAKE HER?
WHY? YOU WOULDN'T WANT TO KEEP HER, AN OLD BACHELOR LIKE YOU!
I'M A LONE THING, MASTER GODFREY--AND SO IS SHE! MY MONEY'S GONE. I DON'T KNOW WHERE--AND THIS HAS COME FROM I DON'T KNOW WHERE!
TORN BETWEEN HIS PATERNAL DUTY TOWARDS THE CHILD AND HIS LOVE FOR NANCY, GODFREY LEFT MARNER'S COTTAGE AND RETURNED TO RED HOUSE...

AMONG THE NOTABLE MOTHERS WHO CAME TO OFFER ADVICE TO SILAS MARNER, DOLLY WINTHROP WAS THE ONE WHOSE OFFICES WERE MOST ACCEPTABLE TO THE OLD MAN...

MASTER GODFREY LEFT ME A HALF GUINEA TO BUY SOME CLOTHES FOR THE CHILD!

THERE'S NO NEED TO BUY MORE THAN A PAIR OF SHOES! I'VE GOT SOME PETTICOATS THAT AARON WORE FIVE YEARS AGO!

TRUE TO HER WORD, DOLLY RETURNED THE SAME DAY WITH HER BUNDLE...

YOU MUST BE CAREFUL, MASTER MARNER, NOT TO LET THE LITTLE ANGEL WANDER OFF WHILE YOU'RE AT YOUR WORK!

I'LL TIE HER TO THE LEG OF THE LOOM! TIE HER WITH A GOOD LONG STRIP OF SOMETHING.

HAVING ATTENDED TO THE CHILD, DOLLY SPOKE TO MARNER ABOUT HER FUTURE...

IF YOU DO THE RIGHT THING BY THE CHILD, MASTER MARNER, YOU MUST TAKE HER TO THE CHURCH AND HAVE HER CHRISTENED!

MARNER'S FACE FLUSHED A MOMENT UNDER A NEW ANXIETY...
WHAT IS IT YOU MEAN BY "CHRISTENED." WON'T FOLKS BE GOOD TO HER WITHOUT IT?
DEAR, DEAR, MASTER MARNER! HAD YOU NO FATHER NOR MOTHER WHO TAUGHT YOU TO SAY YOUR PRAYERS?
YES, I USED TO KNOW A GREAT DEAL ABOUT THAT-- BUT YOUR WAYS ARE DIFFERENT! MY COUNTRY WAS A GOOD WAY OFF.
BUT I'LL TAKE HER TO CHURCH, MRS. WINTHROP! IF YOU THINK IT'S THE RIGHT THING FOR THE CHILD, I'LL TAKE HER THERE AND HAVE HER CHRISTENED!
LATER...
TAKE GOOD CARE OF THE ANGEL, MASTER MARNER! I'LL ASK MR. MACEY TO SPEAK TO THE PARSON ABOUT THE CHRISTENING.
NEXT DAY, THE CHILD WAS BAPTIZED AND NAMED EPPIE, AFTER SILAS MARNER'S YOUNGER SISTER...

IT WAS A BRIGHT AUTUMN SUNDAY, SIXTEEN YEARS AFTER SILAS MARNER HAD FOUND EPPIE ON HIS HEARTH...

MORNING SERVICES AT RAVELOE WERE ENDED...

GODFREY CASS AND NANCY LAMMETER HAD NOW BEEN MARRIED FOR SIX YEARS...

I TRUST, BROTHER GODFREY, YOU AND MRS. CASS ENJOYED THE SERVICES.

THEY WERE MOST IMPRESSIVE, PARSON!

AH, BROTHER SILAS! I MUST SAY OUR EPPIE BECOMES MORE CHARMING WITH THE YEARS!

THANK YOU PARSON!

EPPIE STOLE A SLY GLANCE AT YOUNG AARON WINTHROP TRAILING ALONG BEHIND...

I WISH WE HAD A LITTLE GARDEN WITH DOUBLE DAISIES IN, LIKE MRS. WINTHROP!

ONLY IT'D TAKE A DEAL OF DIGGING AND BRINGING FRESH SOIL--AND IT 'UD BE TOO HARD WORK FOR YOU, FATHER.
I CAN DIG FOR YOU, MASTER MARNER! IT'LL BE PLAY FOR ME WHEN I'M THROUGH WITH MY DAY'S WORK! I COULD BRING YOU SOME SOIL FROM MR. CASS'S GARDEN!
AARON, M'LAD, I DIDN'T KNOW YOU WERE THERE! WELL, IF YOU COULD HELP ME WITH THE DIGGING, WE MIGHT GET HER A BIT 'O GARDEN ALL THE SOONER!
EPPIE CHIMED IN, HALF BASHFULLY AND HALF ROGUISHLY. . .
I SHOULDN'T HA' SAID ANYTHING ABOUT IT, FATHER. ONLY MRS. WINTHROP SAID AARON WOULD BE SO GOOD AS. . .
AND YOU MIGHT HA' KNOWN IT WITHOUT MOTHER TELLING YOU. I'M ABLE AND WILLING TO DO A GOOD TURN FOR MASTER MARNER.

AS AARON TURNED BACK TO THE VILLAGE, SILAS AND EPPIE CONTINUED UP THE SHELTERED LANE...
OH, DADDY! I DON'T THINK I SHALL WANT ANYTHING ELSE WHEN WE'VE GOT A LITTLE GARDEN! AND I KNEW AARON WOULD DIG IT FOR US!
YOU'RE A DEEP LITTLE PUSS, YOU ARE! BUT YOU'LL MAKE YOURSELF FINE AND BEHOLDEN TO AARON!
COME, COME, LET ME CARRY YOUR PRAYER BOOK, ELSE YOU'LL BE DROPPING IT JUMPING THAT WAY!
OH, NO, I SHAN'T! HE LIKES IT!
SEVERAL DAYS LATER...
FATHER, IF I WAS TO BE MARRIED, OUGHT I TO BE MARRIED WITH MY MOTHER'S RING?
WHY, EPPIE! HA', YOU BEEN THINKIN' ON IT?
ONLY THIS LAST WEEK, FATHER, SINCE AARON TALKED TO ME ABOUT IT!
SILAS WAS FEARFUL OF LOSING EPPIE, BUT PROMISED TO SPEAK TO MRS. WINTHROP ABOUT IT...

LATER... ONE SUNDAY IN THE CHILDLESS HOME OF GODFREY AND NANCY CASS...
IS YOUR MASTER COME INTO THE YARD, JANE?
NO, MA'AM, HE ISN'T!
BUT THERE'S FOLKS MAKING HASTE ALL ONE WAY AFORE THE FRONT WINDOW! I HOPE NOBODY'S HURT, THAT'S ALL!
THAT GIRL'S ALWAYS TERRIFYING ME! I WISH GODFREY WOULD COME IN!
SOON...
DEAR, I'M SO THANKFUL YOU'RE COME! I WAS BEGINNING TO GET...
IT-IT ISN'T FATHER...
NANCY, I'VE HAD A GREAT SHOCK! BUT I CARE MOST ABOUT THE SHOCK IT'LL BE TO YOU!
TREMBLING WITH EMOTION, GODFREY TOLD NANCY THAT THE SKELETON OF HIS MISSING BROTHER DUNSTAN HAD JUST BEEN FOUND, TOGETHER WITH THE MONEY WHICH HAD BEEN STOLEN FROM SILAS MARNER SIXTEEN YEARS BEFORE IN THE STONE-PITS. GODFREY THEN REVEALED THE GREAT SECRET WHICH HE HAD KEPT TO HIMSELF FOR OVER SIXTEEN YEARS, THE SECRET THAT EPPIE WAS IN REALITY HIS CHILD AND THAT MOLLY FARREN, THE WOMAN FOUND FROZEN TO DEATH NEAR THE STONE-PITS, HAD BEEN HIS WIFE.

THERE WAS NO INDIGNATION IN NANCY'S VOICE AS SHE SPOKE . . . ONLY DEEP REGRET . . .
GODFREY, IF YOU HAD ONLY TOLD ME SIXTEEN YEARS AGO, WE COULD HAVE DONE THE RIGHT THING BY THE CHILD.
BUT YOU WOULDN'T HAVE MARRIED ME, DARLING, IF I HAD TOLD YOU! WITH YOUR PRIDE, AND YOUR FATHER'S, YOU WOULD HAVE HATED HAVING ANYTHING TO DO WITH ME!
NANCY ASSURED GODFREY THAT SHE WOULD NEVER HAVE MARRIED ANYONE ELSE. GODFREY ENTREATED HER TO ADOPT EPPIE AS THEIR CHILD. SHE WAS AT FIRST RELUCTANT, BUT FINALLY GAVE IN . . .
THAT EVENING, WITHOUT DISCLOSING HIS RELATIONSHIP TO EPPIE, GODFREY OFFERED TO ADOPT HER . . .
MARNER! NANCY AND I WISH TO ADOPT EPPIE!
EH! WHAT'S THIS?
WE'VE COME TO TAKE EPPIE AWAY FROM THIS DRAB EXISTENCE AND BRING HER UP IN A MANNER MORE FITTING WITH A . . . WITH A GIRL OF HER ACCOMPLISHMENTS!
FOR A MOMENT, SILAS SAT THERE TREMBLING WITH EMOTION, THEN . . .
EPPIE MY CHILD, SPEAK! I WON'T STAND IN YOUR WAY! THANK MR. AND MRS. CASS!

HER CHEEKS FLUSHED, BUT NOT WITH SHYNESS THIS TIME, EPPIE STEPPED FORWARD, DROPPING A LOW COURTESY TO THEIR VISITORS. . .
THANK YOU, MA'AM! THANK YOU, SIR!
BUT I CAN'T LEAVE MY FATHER AND I DON'T WANT TO BE A LADY! I COULD NOT GIVE UP THE FOLKS I'VE BEEN USED TO!
BUT I HAVE A CLAIM ON YOU, EPPIE!--THE STRONGEST OF ALL CLAIMS! MARNER, EPPIE IS MY CHILD--HER MOTHER WAS MY WIFE!
RELIEVED BY EPPIE'S REPLY, MARNER RETORTED FIERCELY. . .
THEN, SIR, WHY DIDN'T YOU SAY SO SIXTEEN YEARS AGO? WHY DID YOU NOT CLAIM HER BEFORE I LEARNED TO LOVE HER, INSTEAD OF COMING TO ME NOW WHEN YOU MIGHT AS WELL TAKE MY HEART!
I KNOW THAT, MARNER--I WAS WRONG! I'VE REPENTED OF MY CONDUCT IN THAT MATTER.

"I'M GLAD TO HEAR IT, SIR! BUT REPENTANCE DOESN'T ALTER WHAT HAS BEEN GOING ON FOR SIXTEEN YEARS! IT'S ME SHE'S BEEN CALLING HER FATHER EVER SINCE SHE COULD SAY THE WORD!"

"I MUST WARN YOU, MARNER, YOU'RE PUTTING YOURSELF IN THE WAY OF THE CHILD'S WELFARE! I'M SORRY TO HURT YOU, AFTER WHAT YOU'VE DONE--BUT I MUST INSIST ON TAKING CARE OF MY OWN DAUGHTER!"

GODFREY'S WORDS HAD THEIR EFFECT ON MARNER...

"I'LL SAY NO MORE! LET IT BE AS YOU WILL! SPEAK TO THE CHILD--I'LL HINDER NOTHING!"

"EPPIE, MY DEAR, SAY YOU WILL COME WITH US! YOU'LL HAVE THE BEST OF MOTHERS IN MY WIFE--THAT'LL BE A BLESSING TO YOU ALWAYS!"

"MY DEAR, YOU'LL BE A TREASURE TO ME--WE SHALL WANT FOR NOTHING WHEN WE HAVE OUR DAUGHTER!"

EPPIE DID NOT CURTSY AS SHE DID BEFORE. GRASPING SILAS'S HAND FIRMLY IN HERS, SHE SPOKE OUT IN COLDER DECISION...

"THANK YOU BOTH FOR YOUR OFFERS! BUT I SHALL NEVER BE HAPPY WITHOUT BEING HERE WITH MY FATHER, NO MATTER HOW HUMBLE THE SURROUNDINGS! AS LONG AS HE LIVES, NOBODY SHALL EVER COME BETWEEN US!"

"BUT YOU MUST MAKE SURE, EPPIE! YOU'VE MADE YOUR CHOICE TO STAY AMONG POOR PEOPLE WHEN YOU MIGHT HA' HAD EVERYTHING OF THE BEST!"

"I CAN NEVER BE SORRY, FATHER! WHAT COULD I CARE FOR THINGS I'VE NEVER BEEN USED TO! I BELONG HERE WITH YOU!"

THEIR PLEAS HAVING FALLEN ON DEAF EARS, GODFREY AND NANCY TOOK THEIR LEAVE AND RETURNED TO RED HOUSE...

NEXT MORNING...

"EPPIE, THERE'S A LITTLE TRIP I'VE ALWAYS WANTED TO TAKE WITH YOU, AND NOW THAT MY MONEY'S BEEN RETURNED, I THINK WE'LL MAKE A LITTLE BUNDLE OF THINGS AND SET OUT!"

"WHERE TO DADDY?"

TO MY OLD COUNTRY. . . TO THE TOWN WHERE I WAS BORN. . . UP LANTERN YARD! I WANT TO SEE MR. PASTON, THE MINISTER. . .THEY MAY HAVE FOUND SOMETHING TO CLEAR ME OF THE ROBBERY!
OH, DADDY, THAT WOULD BE WONDERFUL! IT'LL BE GOOD TO GET AWAY FROM RAVELOE FOR A BIT!
FOUR DAYS LATER, SILAS AND EPPIE FOUND THEMSELVES ON THE STREETS OF A GREAT MANUFACTURING TOWN, IN THE VICINITY OF LANTERN YARD. . .
I HARDLY RECOGNIZE THE PLACE, EPPIE! IT'S YEARS SINCE I LEFT LANTERN YARD!
WHY NOT ASK THIS MAN THE WAY TO THE YARD?
HE WOULDN'T KNOW! GENTLE-FOLK DIDN'T EVER GO UP TO THE YARD! I'LL ASK THE WAY TO PRISON STREET. . . THAT'S WHERE THE JAIL IS! I KNOW MY WAY OUT O' THAT AS IF I'D SEEN IT YESTERDAY.

THEY ARRIVED AT THE JAIL-HOUSE...
THERE IT IS, EPPIE! THAT'S JUST THE SAME! IT'S THE THIRD TURNING ON THE LEFT FROM HERE!
OH, WHAT A DARK PLACE! IS LANTERN YARD LIKE THIS, FATHER?
MY PRECIOUS CHILD! IT ISN'T A BIG STREET LIKE THIS! I NEVER WAS EASY IN THIS STREET MYSELF! BUT I WAS FOND OF LANTERN YARD!
JOURNEY'S END, AT LAST...
DEAR HEART! WHY, THERE'RE PEOPLE COMING OUT O' THE YARD AS IF THEY'D BEEN AT CHAPEL AT THIS TIME O' DAY--A WEEK-DAY NOON!
FOR MINUTES, SILAS STOOD WRAPPED IN DISTANT MEMORIES AND AMAZED AT THE CHANGE THAT HAD COME OVER HIS FORMER HOME...
FATHER, WHAT'S THE MATTER?
IT'S GONE, CHILD! LANTERN YARD'S GONE. I SHALL NEVER KNOW NOW WHETHER THEY GOT AT THE TRUTH OF THE ROBBERY!

EPPIE WAS FEARFUL LEST ONE OF HER FATHER'S STRANGE ATTACKS SHOULD COME ON...
COME INTO THAT LITTLE BRUSH SHOP AND SIT DOWN, FATHER! PERHAPS THE PEOPLE CAN TELL YOU SOMETHING ABOUT IT!
BRUSH SHOP
IN THE BRUSH SHOP...
SORRY, STRANGER! I NEVER HEARD OF MR. PASTON OR ANY OF THOSE OTHER PEOPLE YOU MENTIONED! THE FACTORY WAS ALREADY BUILT WHEN I CAME HERE!
THEIR QUEST ENDED, MARNER AND EPPIE RETURNED TO RAVELOE. MARNER WAS RESIGNED TO THE FACT THAT HE WOULD NEVER KNOW WHETHER OR NOT HIS NAME HAD BEEN CLEARED IN LANTERN YARD.
SOME TIME LATER WHEN THE GREAT LILACS AND LABURNUMS IN THE OLD-FASHIONED GARDENS OF RAVELOE SHOWED THEIR GOLDEN AND PURPLE WEALTH, PREPARATIONS WERE MADE FOR THE MARRIAGE OF EPPIE AND AARON WINTHROP.
THE BELLS IN THE CHURCH BELFRY RANG OUT MERRILY...
WHAT'S THE OCCASION, DEACON, A WEDDIN'?
A WEDDING INDEED! IT'S THE MARNER GIRL AND YOUNG AARON WINTHROP!
IN SILAS MARNER'S COTTAGE...
I'LL BE TWICE BLESSED-- AND THE HAPPIEST MAN IN RAVELOE!
YOU WON'T BE GIVING ME AWAY, FATHER! YOU'LL BE TAKING AARON TO BE A SON TO YOU!

THE CEREMONY ENDED, THE WEDDING PROCESSION RETURNED FROM THE CHURCH. . .
MR. MACEY'S LOOKING FOR A WORD FROM US! HE'LL BE HURT IF WE PASS HIM AND SAY NOTHING!
WELL, MASTER MARNER, I'VE LIVED TO SEE MY WORDS COME TRUE! I WAS THE FIRST TO SAY THERE WAS NO HARM IN YOU. . . AND I WAS THE FIRST TO SAY YOU'D GET YOUR MONEY BACK! GOOD LUCK!
EPPIE AND HER HUSBAND WENT TO LIVE WITH SILAS MARNER AT THE COTTAGE WHICH HAD BEEN FIXED OVER AT THE EXPENSE OF GODFREY CASS TO SUIT SILAS' LARGER FAMILY. . .
OH, FATHER! WHAT A PRETTY HOME OURS IS! I THINK NOBODY COULD BE HAPPIER THAN WE ARE!
TEARS WELLED IN OLD MARNER'S EYES AT THE REALIZATION THAT HE WAS TO SHARE EPPIE'S HAPPINESS IN THE FEW REMAINING YEARS ALLOTTED TO HIM. . .
The END

SILAS MARNER

GEORGE ELIOT

Silas Marner is one of those rare novels which becomes an emblem for an idea. A fairy tale without the fairies, this short novel represents George Eliot's vision of a moral order in which the good and honest working man triumphs after long suffering. A victim of prejudice and betrayal, Silas Marner takes false comfort, first in his weaving, then in the gold the weaving earns him. When accident conspires to take his precious gold from him, Marner is bereft until a small child wanders into his tiny shack and tiny life. Marner finds himself redeemed by his love for the child, Eppie; in time, Eppie repays Silas Marner for all his losses many times over. Though perhaps not as impressive a work of literature as George Eliot's more ponderous novels, such as *Middlemarch* and *Adam Bede*, *Silas Marner* has a simplicity of narration and a purity of conception which has earned it many enthusiasts in the century-and-a-half since its publication. It remains most readers' first introduction to Eliot, herself a writer emblematic of the social, religious and intellectual changes which shaped nineteenth-century England.

THE AUTHOR

George Eliot was a woman of many identities, and her life makes up a large part of her reputation as a writer. In both her personal and professional lives, she bucked the prevailing tide. At a time when England was the dominant nation on the planet, she lived overseas. She conducted many well-known affairs with married men, though moral rectitude and obedience to the social norm were widely believed to be the reasons for Britain's international success. Most women's lives were defined by their fathers, their looks and their husbands—few women could own property or maintain any sort of independent public identity—but Eliot cultivated an independent image based on the quality of her mind, not the status of her family or the beauty of her appearance. Common wisdom held that the British Empire was created on the playing fields of England's great private schools, which only the rich attended; but George Eliot wrote about the virtues of the working class. Eliot praised the community spirit and bedrock morality found in Britain's small towns, while industrialization brought thousands into the large cities from the English countryside. She was a brilliant woman, drawn to bring her full intellect to oppose any idea which she believed was imposed by society rather than from an individual's mind.

Born November 22, 1819, Mary Anne Evans was Robert Evans' fifth child to survive infancy, the third child by his second wife. Robert Evans had trained as a carpenter, but had become a real success by his astute management of a large estate. The acres of farmland and forest on the Newdigate-Parker estate had long provided the noble family who owned it with a heady income; the development of coal reserves in the early 18th-century had turned it into a fortune. During Robert Evans' stewardship of the estate, the ownership of that fortune remained uncertain, as branches of the family sued one another for their rightful piece of the pie. Young Mary Anne grew up in a fine house on the estate, watching her father manage property, not for any particular owner, but to generate the greatest income possible from the land, as though this were a virtue which served the nation itself. He never rose above the working-class to which he was born, but Robert Evans supported the politics and principles of the upper classes, and believed strongly in a rigidly structured society. He raised his children to take their places in it.

For young Mary Anne, blessed with a startling mind but a homely face, that meant school. Women rarely received any formal education in those days, but Mary Anne's capacities sparked a commitment to serious study; it's possible too, that Mary Anne's parents worried that her appearance would make marriage less likely for her. An education would suit her for one of the few careers open to women, that of teacher or governess. Mary Anne quickly picked up foreign languages and was reading books of great seriousness at age 12. Unfortunately, not long after, both Mary Ann's parents became ill, her mother terminally so. Mary Ann withdrew from school and came home to nurse her family. Her partial education at a Christian school and her stressful situation resulted in her conversion to "evangelical" Christianity (see **Church, Chapel and Evangelism**), which faith sustained her through her mother's death and her father's recovery. As her older siblings married and began families of their own, it became clear that Mary Anne was expected to become her father's companion and nurse in his old age, much like Priscilla Lammeter in *Silas Marner*.

This no doubt would have been her life if chance had not thrown her in with some local eccentrics in Coventry, where she had spent her youth. Now just over 20, Mary Anne had lost her adolescent enthusiasm for religion. Fearful that her isolation from education would make her stupid, she continued reading voraciously, with a particular interest in recent scientific discoveries and their effects on the Biblical conception of the world. Her curiosity about what sort of world would replace the God-ordered Christian one of prior centuries led her to Charles and Cara Bray, a radical thinking—and living—couple with a circle of equally progressive friends. Charles Bray had recently publish his *Philosophy of Necessity*, which put forward the idea that life could be predetermined even without a God to do the predetermining; Nature could order life. Cara Bray's brother, Charles Hennell, had also offered a treatise questioning religion, the influential *Inquiry into the*

Church, Chapel and Evangelism

The church to which Silas Marner belongs in Lantern Yard appears to be one of the evangelical Church of England congregations. While the Church of England was overwhelmingly the national church of Britain (until the 1850s you had to be a member of the Church of England in order to get a degree at Oxford or Cambridge, for example), not everyone in the nation was a member; and the church itself was divided into High and Low Church members. High Church believers tended to favor the social status quo, including clergy who might not take their duties ultra-seriously. As time went on, High Church also came to mean more chanting, more ritual, more of the practices that had been thrown out during the Reformation—on the theory that these more Catholic rituals helped the Church to maintaining a dignified distance from the people. Quite the opposite, Low Church believers wanted a church that was less concerned with pomp and ceremony (and with maintaining class differences) and more concerned with man's inherently sinful nature. The Low Church, or Evangelical, believers did not want to see colored vestments on the clergy, or to hear sermons or prayers "intoned"—nor did they hold with singing, dancing, hunting, or partying, particularly on the part of the clergy! Life was serious, hard work for the lower classes in Britain, and they wanted a Church that reflected that seriousness.

Indeed, class played a big part in Victorian religion. The upper and middle classes concerned themselves with issues of High and Low Church. But the poor and working class were at least as likely to be Methodists, a sect started in the 1700s by John Wesley. This was grim, hellfire and damnation religion based in back-to-the-Bible seriousness—and an egalitarian message that said that salvation wasn't based in who you were, but in what you did. Many Methodists continued in that faith even as they moved up the class ladder. But as some climbed, they joined the more acceptable Church of England... some even became High Church.

Origins of Christianity, which Mary Anne found significant. In an early signal of her changing mind, the future George Eliot changed her name for the first time by dropping the 'e' from Mary Anne.

Her involvement with this crew of radicals put Mary Ann on a collision course with her father, a crash which occurred in the winter and spring of 1842, when Mary Ann was 22 years old. She had lost her faith, she claimed, and couldn't attend church without feeling like a hypocrite. Robert Evans threatened to cut her off without a home or money if she did not continue her duties as his daughter, including accompanying him to church. The conflict lasted several months and drove home to Mary Ann the precariousness of women's lives in early Victorian England. Without money of her own, and with an unfinished education, Mary Ann could not long survive without the support of her family. She returned to her father's house, and to his church, but determined to pursue even more actively the alternative life which the Brays represented and which her father abhorred.

The Brays, the Hennells and also the Brabants, another family of progressives, formed May Ann's intellectual circle and offered both a philosophy and a life in utter contrast to that in her father's house. These people believed that public education should be available to everyone, not only to those who accepted the Church of England. They regarded the Bible as the work of human brings, not of God, and were uncertain of the historical reality of Jesus Christ. They believed that science would answer more questions about the nature of our world than a hundred religions could, and advocated scientific approaches to education, to social organization, and to government. They also believed in open marriages, in communally raised children, and in small-scale communities in which people looked out for one another rather than for their own interests. Although it is clear that Mary Ann adopted many of the ideas circulating in this group, it isn't clear how much she put them into action; it's possible that she engaged in sexual relationships with several members.

Mary Ann Evans occupied the remainder of her time with taking care of her father, aiding the poor, and translating philosophical and scientific texts from German into English. After her father's death, when she was 29, Mary Ann moved to London, where to became an editor at the liberal *Westminster Review*. Her work at the journal put her at the center of progressive intellectual life at a time when European ideology was in turmoil. Political and economic upheaval rocked most countries in Europe, and many progressives felt that they occupied the moral center of these enormous changes. Eliot presently changed her name again, this time to Marian, and found herself in the thick of the movement with both her contributions to the *Westminster Review* and her romantic ties with Herbert Spencer, the grandfather of modern sociology, and George Henry Lewes, a sort of intellectual man-about-town. Much to Marian's disappointment, Spencer couldn't work up an emotional interest in her, and she fell into a companionship with Lewes as a result Spencer's determined romantic disinteres

Their relationship suffered from one central problem: Lewes was already mar

Fate and George Eliot

One of the most curious aspects of *Silas Marner* is the working out of Fate in the novel. Godfrey Cass is Fate's most fortunate son. As the novel begins, he is trapped in a marriage he doesn't want. His brother Dunstan uses the secret of the marriage to blackmail Godfrey into behavior he loathes, and he is thus in the process of losing both his good reputation and the faith of his father. Then two accidental deaths bring about Godfrey's release. First, Dunstan falls into the stone-pit and dies; then Molly Farren, his secret wife, collapses in a drug-induced stupor and freezes to death. Without these lucky breaks, Godfrey's life would head south; his father would probably end up making good on his threat to marry again and make a more deserving heir. But in the novel everything works out for Godfrey. He returns to his former moral life, regains his father's respect, and marries the woman of his dreams. Despite these things, his life is a shambles. He and Nancy can produce no children. Nancy is nervous and frequently unwell; Godfrey is obsessed with his failure to claim the beautiful Eppie as his own, just as he is tormented by the knowledge that his own success has depended on the unfortunate deaths of two people whom he had once loved.

For Silas Marner, fate seems an enemy. First, the drawing of lots at Lantern Yard shows him to be guilty of a crime he did not commit. Then an unknown robber takes from him the only thing he values: his gold. Even the arrival of Eppie at his hearth can hardly be seen as the happy deliverance of Fate; only the fact that Silas Marner takes the child as Fate's replacement of his lost fortune makes her seem anything but a burden to him. No one in Raveloe would have thought any less of him if he had turned the girl over to the parish instead of raising her himself. At the end of the novel, when he gets his stolen money back, he seems entirely indifferent to it, having found something of greater value.

Silas Marner, then, can be read as a treatise against wishing. Fate smiles on Godfrey Cass. He gets everything he desires; but his life isn't worth living. Silas get nothing he desires, but ends up happy anyway. For George Eliot, this is more than simple irony, but fundamental truth: human beings don't know enough about the workings of life to wish wisely. When Fate deals a crushing blow, it may defeat you, but it also may only serve to turn your attention to the very thing you needed. When Eliot stepped away from England, in a relationship with a married man, she couldn't have realized it was the first step on a path which would bring her greatness. By the time she had written *Silas Marner*, she had good reason to believe that only Fate knows the irregular paths a human life might follow.

ried, though his wife had another lover who was the father of the Lewes children. In other ways, though, her alliance with Lewes was fortuitous; it is uncertain whether she would have taken the bold step of writing fiction if it had not been for Lewes. Though indispensable at the *Westminster Review*, Marian did little creative work while engaged there. George Henry Lewes encouraged her to express her own ideas instead of merely translating books she admired. In 1854, with Marian on the verge of beginning a new, creative life and Lewes unwilling to carry on a divided existence, the pair moved to Germany, where they set up house as a married couple.

Over the next decade, George Eliot became a popular novelist and a cultural force through half a dozen books, including *Adam Bede*, *The Mill on the Floss* and *Silas Marner*. Marian at first insisted on keeping her identity a secret, perhaps out of fear that readers wouldn't take a woman's stories seriously, perhaps in fear of failure, or perhaps as a simple protection of her privacy. Her elopement with Lewes was well-known in intellectual circles, and that knowledge could well have influenced the reception of her fiction. In any case, she found writing fiction very much to her liking. It also paid well: for the first time in her life, Mary Anne Evans had her own money, and her independence. It is testimony to the strength of her love for Lewes that despite this new freedom she stayed with him until his death, often going by the name Mrs. Lewes, and frequently playing stepmother to his legal wife's children. Often, Marian had to give Lewes money to keep his wife out of debt.

In 1860, when she composed *Silas Marner*, George Eliot had intended to write another novel, an historical romance called *Romola*. The story of the miserly weaver, however, possessed her so strongly that she wrote it almost without thinking, following the story rather than forming it. Though the book is peculiarly short compared to most novels of that time, and the subject and style almost Gothicly strange, the book became an instant success. Her identity by now widely known and accepted, George Eliot's unusual lifestyle and transgender name did nothing to inhibit her fame, but rather contributed to it. She published many more novels, including *Middlemarch* and *Daniel Deronda*. After Lewes' death in 1878, she married an old friend, John Cross. She died within a year of this marriage. George Eliot—Marian Lewes, Mary Anne Evans or whatever one chooses to call her—was an important cultural figure until the end of her life.

CHARACTERS

Silas Marner: *a self-employed weaver*

Raveloe

Though not a person, the town of Raveloe is perhaps the most important character in the George Eliot's *Silas Marner*. In many ways, the book is less about what happens to the title character than about what happens to Raveloe in the course of thirty years. The book opens with a description of the place, and Eliot marks each transition in the novel—when the sixteen years pass, for example, or as the wedding begins—with a description of the town as a whole. She notes its isolation from the world; it lies an hour from any main road, and since it is rich enough to support itself, the town pursues no further contact. The changes that takes place in Raveloe and in Silas Marner take place as though on an island. In the novel, Marner is the only person who travels beyond Raveloe and its neighboring places, searching for something Raveloe can't provide. Though he undergoes a vast transformation from a miserly and closed-hearted man to a generous and loving one, Raveloe experiences as large a makeover.

In describing Raveloe's fear of Marner at the beginning of the book, George Eliot noted, "How was a man to be explained unless you at least knew somebody who knew his father and mother?" He is a stranger to a place which had rarely known strangers. In fact, the men at the Rainbow often repeat the story of one stranger who came to town before, several generations earlier: Nancy Lammeter's grandfather. But about him the town agrees "it was soon seen as we'd got a new parish'ner as know'd the rights and customs o' things." Silas Marner is no such man, and the peace of Raveloe can't be restored until he become fully enrolled as a member of the community. Raveloe's suspicion of Silas Marner gives way to faith in him because, in raising Eppie, he has given the best proof that he is a worthy citizen of the place. In some ways, all the stories in *Silas Marner* take place because of the difficulty Raveloe has in integrating the stranger into its insular life.

William Dane: *Silas' best friend in his home town, Lantern Yard (See previous page)*

Sarah: *engaged to Silas in Lantern Yard*

Squire Cass: *Raveloe's major landholder, who presides at the Red House*

Godfrey Cass: *the eldest of four Cass sons, and thought to be the best*

Dunstan Cass: *the second son, a rogue*

Nancy Lammeter: *the daughter of a prominent Raveloe family, and the woman Godfrey Cass wants to marry*

> SUPPOSE, NOW, YOU GET THE MONEY YOURSELF AND SAVE ME THE TROUBLE! IT WAS YOUR BROTHERLY LOVE, YOU KNOW, THAT MADE YOU LEND IT TO ME!

Molly Farren: *Godfrey's secret and lamented wife, and mother of his young daughter; a drug addict*

Priscilla Lammeter: *Nancy's homely sister*

Mr. Lammeter: *Nancy and Priscilla's father, a widower, formerly married to an Osgood daughter*

The Osgoods: *Raveloe's second family*

Doctor Kimble: *the Raveloe physician*

Bryce: *a wealthy neighbor of the Casses, prospective buyer of Godfrey's best horse, Wildfire*

Sally Oates: *the Raveloe cobbler's wife, whom Marner cures with herbs*

John Snell: *proprietor of the Rainbow, Raveloe's pub*

Jem Rodney: *a Raveloe poacher*

Mr. Macey: *a tailor and the clerk of the parish in Raveloe*

Tookey, Winthrop, Dowlas, Bob the butcher: *the various tradesmen at Raveloe, who gather at night at the Rainbow*

Dolly Winthrop: *the wheelwright's wife, mother to Aaron, friend and adviser to Silas Marner*

Kench: *the town constable*
Mr. Crackenthorpe: *rector of the parish*

Justice Malam: *Raveloe's judge*

Hephzibah Marner called **Eppie:** *Godfrey Cass' and Molly Farren's daughter, raised by Silas Marner*

Aaron Winthrop: *Dolly's son and, eventually, Eppie's suitor*

PLOT

The story of *Silas Marner* lends itself particularly well to the Classics Illustrated format: the action is simple and direct, and the moments of highest drama also move the story forward. The death of Molly Farren and Silas Marner's discovery of the young child on his hearth, provide crucial twists in the story, and also lend themselves very well to illustration. Following George

Riding to Hounds

The fox hunt in which Dunstan Cass destroys his brother's horse is one of the dramatic moments in *Silas Marner*. But for most American readers, the tradition of 'riding to hounds' is wreathed in mystery. Originally, fox hunting wasn't even a sport, it was a necessity: foxes destroyed livestock and, like rats, they were hunted for rewards paid by church wardens. What the gentry hunted for sport were deer—until the deer population got too scarce. At which point someone had the bright idea to hunt foxes. This meant breeding faster, wilier dogs to keep up with the foxes. When, in the 1700s, dogs began to match the speed of their prey, fox-hunting really took off. And how exactly does a fox hunt work?

The first Monday of November was, traditionally, the first day of fox-hunting season. Very early on the morning of a hunt, workers went out to block up foxholes in the hunt area, cutting off escape for the intended victim (foxes are nocturnal; the idea was that they would stagger home after a night's foraging to find that the door was, in effect, locked). Around midday, the hunters and pack (40 or so dogs) gathered. A huntsman (the guy who handled the dogs) went off with the dogs with the riders following, to flush a fox out of the bush or thicket in which it was hiding. The first hunter who saw the fox yelled "Tally-Ho!" Then the whole concern—fox, dogs, and hunters—chased hell-for-leather over the countryside. Eventually the fox was cornered, and torn limb from limb, by the hounds. The dogs would eat everything except the head, paws, and tail (called the mask, pads, and brush, respectively) which were awarded as hunt trophies to the lead riders. After the meet there were often picnics and dances to round out the event. Dashing over fields and through rivers was probably great fun for everyone concerned—except the fox!

Eliot's plot with great fidelity, this adaptation takes few liberties (although it leaves out some of the history of Raveloe, history which makes the small town come to life in the novel). These small omissions are of great importance in understanding the book, however. The true hero of Eliot's book is the village community; he Classics Illustrated adaptation attempts to fashion Silas Marner himself into the story's hero, and must misrepresent the story to do so.

But Silas Marner *is* the story's most dominant character. His life in Lantern Yard, where he lived before coming to Raveloe, drives his actions throughout the novel bearing his name. Lantern Yard is a small place, like Raveloe, occupying only a part of a larger town. It is poor, almost strangled, and it offers its inhabitants very little solace but church. The people of the Yard are of an evangelical religious conviction (as Mary Anne Evans was when she was a teenager). The tightness of this community opens Silas to betrayal by William Dane, his closest friend. Dane steals money belonging to the church and plants the bag which had contained the money—not the money itself, as one CI illustration implies — at Silas' house, (See next page) probably to destroy his friend's reputation and gain Sarah, Silas' betrothed, for himself. The church community votes to shun him, and Silas Marner takes to the road. He winds up in Raveloe.

The novel itself opens in Raveloe fifteen years later. Silas is now a man of forty. He has never become a welcome member of the town, for a number of reasons. His long face and protuberant eyes make him look corpse-like, and people don't feel comfortable around him. As a man liable to fits—probably mild epilepsy—the community regards him as peculiar, perhaps enchanted or bedeviled. He has unconsciously added to that reputation by helping cure the heart disease of a woman named Sally Oates; when Dr. Kimble can do nothing to help, an herbal preparation Marner learned from his mother does the trick. People are prepared to accept him as a medicine man, but Silas fears the limits of his own knowledge. "Silas might have driven a profitable trade in charms," Eliot writes, but "he had never known an impulse toward falsity, and he drove one after another away." People come to believe he is simply being cruel in denying them help, rather than honest in knowing his limitations; they don't want him as a part of their community. So Marner uses money to fill the hollowness in his soul caused first by the betrayal at Lantern Yard and then by the coldness of the people of Raveloe.

Money is also at the root of problems in the Cass household: Squire Cass has it and his sons want it. Godfrey, the oldest son and by all accounts the best, would unquestionably be most likely to inherit the estate— except that his behavior lately has gone downhill. The cause is two-fold: first, he is secretly and unfortunately married to Molly Farren; and second, his no-good brother Dunstan is blackmailing him about the marriage. We are given little information about why Godfrey married

Molly in the first place, but we understand why he no longer wants to be tied to her, despite their child: she is addicted to laudanum, an opiate. He now has his heart set on Nancy Lammeter, the best catch in Raveloe. He isn't free to do anything more than court her while Molly is alive—or Dunstan, either, who would ruin his brother's reputation for spite and profit. Dunstan has already cajoled so much money out of his brother that Godfrey owes their father £100. In order to get it, he allows Dunstan to take Wildfire, Godfrey's finest horse, and sell him.

Dunstan sells the horse well, but then, through his foolishness, he forces Wildfire over a staked fence and kills him. Walking back to Raveloe in the dark, Dunstan conceives a plan. Everyone in the town knows that Silas Marner has put away a large sum in gold. If he could be persuaded to loan it to the Cass boys, everyone would make out well. When Dunstan comes to Marner's house by the stone-pits, he finds it empty. Only then does he get the idea of simply taking the gold. He creeps off into the night and disappears.

Silas Marner returns to find his gold gone, an event which forces him into the bloodstream of Raveloe. He runs to the Rainbow, the town pub, and asks for help. The people reach out to him, bring his case before the proper authorities, and offer him advice about why God has seen fit to take away his fortune. But this advice has little effect: Marner lost his faith when the godly community in Lantern Yard cast him out.

Godfrey Cass shows less emotion at his brother's unexplained absence than Marner does at the loss of his gold; his shortage of funds distresses him more. At last, he confesses to his father that he loaned Dunstan the money owed him, though he doesn't explain why. The Squire threatens to disown Godfrey, but in the end just cautions him to stick to a more righteous life, including marrying Nancy Lammeter.

Godfrey would like nothing better, and at a series of parties—Mrs. Osgood's birthday, Christmas, and New Year's Eve—he again courts her unevenly.

(See next page)

On New Year's, though, Raveloe is in for a shock. Tired of being ignored by her high-born husband, Molly Farren takes her young daughter and her drugs and walks to town, planning on crashing the party at the Red House. On her way, she takes a long drink of her lau-

What's a Squire?

Squire Cass is called "the greatest man in Raveloe." We hear the title Squire used, but may have no idea what rank or privilege it implies. In fact, the title Squire had, by George Eliot's time, no legal significance at all—but still carried heaps of social significance. Locally there was usually only one "Squire," who was so called because he was a major local landowner from a family with decades—perhaps centuries—in the neighborhood. Frequently Squires were justices of the peace; as frequently they were unofficial referees in disputes, judges for contests, generally the Big Man in town.

danum, fall under its spell and sinks into the snow. Cold and unable to rouse her mother, the one-year-old sees a light and walks toward it. It is Silas Marner's cabin; she enters and falls asleep by the fire. Marner is there, but in a fit and unaware of his little intruder. Hours later, alert again, he discovers the little girl, whose curls he mistakes for his gold. He realizes soon that the child must have been abandoned. He follows her tracks through the snow and finds the inert body of Molly Farren.

Taking the girl with him, Marner runs to the Red House for the doctor. Godfrey recognizes his child, but says nothing. Instead, he takes a surprisingly active interest in the situation, fetching the doctor's assistant, Dolly Winthrop, and helping carry Molly Farren to Marner's cabin. Of course, he wants to find out if the woman is dead or alive, and realizes his future hangs on the question. If she lives, she will certainly name him as her husband and the father of her child; if she dies, he is free to marry Nancy and begin his life anew—but only if he ignores his natural child. Godfrey gets several lucky breaks: not only is Molly dead, of exposure and an overdose, but Marner insists on raising the child himself. As the weaver says, "My money's gone, I don't know where—and this is come from I don't know where. I know nothing—I'm partly mazed." Furthering Godfrey's luck is the continuing absence of his brother Dunstan, the only other person aware of the secret marriage. He can now marry Nancy, and he does. He also provides some money for the child's upkeep, but people in Raveloe assume it's just reward for Silas Marner's devoted kindness in raising the child, whom he names Eppie.

The plot leaps forward sixteen years now. Eppie is grown into womanhood. She and Silas Marner, the only father she has known, are beloved members of the Raveloe community. They attend church together and all the people admire both Eppie's grace and Silas' parenting. Eppie has almost accepted Aaron Winthrop's proposal of marriage; her only condition is that she not have to leave the only father she has ever known. Silas and Eppie sit by the stone pits discussing the matter and watching the water drain; Godfrey Cass has taken over the land and is preparing it for planting. But the declining water reveals a skeleton. The jewelry nearby reveals it to be Dunstan's remains, and the mystery of the long-ago robbery is solved when Marner's gold is found beside him too.

These events force Godfrey into action. To Nancy, his devoted but childless wife of fifteen years, he confesses his earlier marriage and Eppie's true parentage. They approach Silas and Eppie, proposing to take her in as a full member of the distinguished Cass family and make a lady of her. Eppie refuses, saying, "It 'ud be poor work for me to put on things, and ride in a gig, and in a place at church, as 'ud make them as I'm fond of think me unfitting company for 'em. What could *I* care for then?" Godfrey and Nancy go home disappointed, and the leading man at Raveloe at last comes to realize "there's debt's we can't pay like money debts, by paying extra for the years that have slipped by."

Feeling some of his own debts unpaid, Silas Marner wants to return to Lantern Yard, now thirty years after his departure from the place. Eppie, who knows all about what had happened there, agrees to go with him. **When they get to the town, however, Silas cannot recognize the place.** Like most English cities of the period, this one has grown into a manufacturing center. The population has grown, new buildings have gone up, and there is nothing left of Lantern Yard. The disappointed Marner finds not even a scrap of his past life remains. The sorrow from which he had run so vigorously—and from which he had been running for three decades—is gone as though it had never existed. He can't be discovered, but neither can he be exonerated. They return to Raveloe, where Eppie marries Aaron and Silas lives in happy retirement.

FOR MINUTES, SILAS STOOD WRAPPED IN DISTANT MEMORIES AND AMAZED AT THE CHANGE THAT HAD COME OVER HIS FORMER HOME...

FATHER, WHAT'S THE MATTER?

IT'S GONE, CHILD! LANTERN YARD'S GONE. I SHALL NEVER KNOW NOW WHETHER THEY GOT AT THE TRUTH OF THE ROBBERY!

THEME AND CONTEXT
The Individual and the Community

One of George Eliot's primary concerns in *Silas Marner* is the relationship between the individual and the community. For Eliot, this is a deep philosophical problem, representing two very different visions of human life. On the one hand, there is the absolute good of liberty. Individuals should have the freedom to choose their own lives. Her father's efforts to determine what she should believe about religion persuaded her that no one has the power to command the mind of another. At the same time, the same event pointed out to her that maintaining peace in the community—whether a family or a larger social organization—was also highly desirable. What should one do when individual freedom and social peace cannot co-exist?

This was not an idle question in nineteenth century England. Power, wealth and population were growing so quickly that the society required individuals to take charge: to build a new factory, to start a new business in a distant colony, to undertake a project for the common good. From those who couldn't step to the forefront, society expected obedience. Attempts to organize labor unions in the new factories were met with violence. England shipped thousands and thousands of undesirable individuals to Australia. People who had different ideas about the nature of the common good were subject to harsh treatment and exclusion from society. Silas Marner represents the ideal compromise between the individual and the community, a man who remains true to his own sometimes twisted self, but who capitulates to society in the really important things: in pursuing trade, in seeking justice, and in raising children.

One of the things which makes *Silas Marner* a difficult read is that, at the beginning, none of the characters are particularly likable. John Blackwood, George Eliot's publisher, responded to the first 100 pages of the manuscript by noting the book's "want of brighter lights and some characters of whom one can think with pleasure as fellow creatures." But a large part of the novel is an attempt to distinguish between what is an acceptable life in a community, as lived by the Casses and by Marner, and what is a righteous life. At the beginning of the book Godfrey Cass appears to be a more valuable member of the Raveloe community than Silas Marner. But the appearance of Eppie provides a new filter, a test by which to judge behavior, one which Marner passes with almost carefree ease. Because Marner already cared for something outside himself—money—it was easy for him to show how much he cared for Eppie. The Cass boys seem only concerned with themselves; even the presence of a child doesn't alter Godfrey's selfish, self-involved approach to life.

The Righteous Life

For Eliot, one of the most difficult problems of modern life was how to create moral people without demanding religious allegiance. Once you accept that there may not be a God—or even accept that there are people who won't believe in the same God you believe in—you have lost any broad acceptance of a moral standard. Eliot thought that people could lead righteous lives without a belief in God, but that this change required the establishment of some other inflexible social standards. These standards did not include a monogamous marriage—Eliot's life showed that—but they *did* include making sacrifices for the good of children. Religion in Raveloe is a sort of offhand thing, especially when compared with the kind of church Marner was attached to in Lantern Yard. In *Silas Marner* we find out how difficult it is for one person, cut loose from the moral strictures which dominated his youth, to find his way back to a righteous life without God.

The Power of Forgiveness

George Eliot set great store by forgiveness as a moral value. For her forgiveness wasn't so much a matter of apologizing to those people you might have hurt as finding that feeling of forgiveness in yourself; not something you ask for so much as something you experience. This is clearly the case in the story of Silas Marner. He can't let go of the injustices done him in Lantern Yard. Somehow, the betrayal by William Dane is less disturbing to Marner than the determination by lot of his guilt. Decades later, it is that which bothers him the most; the lottery was supposed to reflect the wisdom of God, and yet it falsely "proved" him guilty by it. As he tells Eppie, one reason he wants to revisit

Eliot's Greek Chorus

In Greek Tragedy, the Chorus played the role of narrator and commentator, giving the audience a sense of what they were supposed to think and feel about the story at hand. The point of the Chorus wasn't so much to make sure the audience got the point, but to establish the community values on which the play was based (for example, the point of *Oedipus* would be lost on a community where people routinely married their parents, without the Chorus to make it clear that in the world of the play, incest is a bad thing).

In *Silas Marner*, this function is served by the men who meet to drink at the Rainbow: Winthrop, Tookey, Lundy, Macey, Dowlas, and Mr. Snell, the landlord of the pub. They comment on the lives of their "betters," the gentry who go to the party at the Red House, for example, and they comment on their friends and neighbors—and on outsiders like Silas Marner— as well. Their conversation defines the community and its values, and helps the reader see the various main characters from the viewpoint of the community.

Unlike the Chorus of Greek tragedy, however, Eliot's Chorus is made up of characters with personalities and lives, people you can imagine going home after a night at the Rainbow to wives like Dolly Winthrop. Like the cast on the sitcom *Cheers*, each of these men is a type—the sarcastic wise-guy, the know-it-all, the old guy, the innocent fall-guy.

The Rainbow, as a setting, also reinforces community standards and, particularly, class distinctions. Eliot notes that the public house was divided into the "bar" on the right hand— where the lower class patrons enjoyed their ale and each other—and the "parlor" on the left—which was used by the gentry. The parlor would have comfortable chairs, pictures on the wall, and other 'gentlemanly' furnishings. The bar, or tap room, was more likely to have a table, benches, and a big open fireplace.

Lantern Yard is to ask his old pastor about this contradiction. (See next page) In the end, though, the disappearance of Lantern Yard makes Marner, and the reader, realize that the weight of the events there is all in Marner's mind. If he can forgive his old community, as he has forgiven the unknown robber of his gold, then he can forgive himself too and move forward with joy. Godfrey Cass, on the other hand, discovers that there are some actions which are beyond forgiveness, such as failing to claim his child. It is a burden he will carry to his grave.

The Past in the Present

For most of the characters in *Silas Marner*, the past has a significant hold on the present; indeed, some characters are incapable of giving up the past in favor of the present. The past serves to ground communities: Raveloe is strongly rooted in its own past; knowing each family's history gives the citizens of the town a sense that they know, and can trust, each other. Lantern Yard, a neighborhood in a much larger manufacturing town, is so *un*-rooted that when Silas returns there after thirty-two years away, the town itself has disappeared without a trace. This disappearance literally forces Silas to give up any last attachment he had to his past there, and to live more fully *now*, with Eppie and Aaron, at the book's end. Making peace with the past allows him to embrace the present.

For individuals in the book, the past may be something to embrace—or escape. Geoffrey, for example, spends the whole book trying to outrun his past, first in the form of his marriage to Molly Farren, and then in the form of Eppie, his child. By the time Geoffrey decides to reclaim his past and claim Eppie for his own, it's too late: she has her own past with Silas, the man who raised her. Her present and past are too dear to her for her to accept Geoffrey's offer. And for characters like Squire Cass, the pull of the past can be so powerful it effectively stops them from growing, changing, living fully in the present.

STUDY QUESTIONS

•*Silas Marner* has been called both a fairy tale and a work of realistic fiction. Is it possible for a book to be both? In what way is *Silas Marner* a fairy tale? What qualities in Eliot's writing make it seem realistic?

•Many of the families depicted in *Silas Marner* have no mothers; those families with two parents are seldom represented as families. Why does George Eliot choose to create these motherless families? What point might she be trying to make?

•Would it have made a better ending if Silas Marner had been able to vindicate himself of the crime at Lantern Yard? Is his emptiness at the end a meaningful conclusion to the story of his life or just a cruel trick on the part of George Eliot?

•In some ways, Dunstan Cass is the most human character in *Silas Marner*. He is so consistently selfish, so determined to pursue his own interests that he in some ways creates a kind of sympathy. Do you think Eliot intended the reader to feel sympathy with Dunstan? If so, what purpose does that sympathy serve in the novel?

•Is Silas Marner a good man? By the end of the novel, he is approaching sixty, and we know a good deal about his life. How do we judge him?

•Eppie comes across in the novel as a prize: she falls into Silas Marner's lap when just a toddler, but when Godfrey and Nancy Cass come to offer her a better life sixteen years later, he feels that perhaps he isn't worthy of keeping her. She is described as "the freshest blossom of youth," beautiful and graceful. She is also highly moral and "does not like to be blameworthy even in small things: you see how neatly her prayer-book is folded in her spotted handkerchief." The idea of a beautiful young woman as a prize contradicts everything else George Eliot stands for. How can you make sense of the contradiction?

•When Godfrey Cass comes to claim Eppie, Marner speaks very strongly to him. "You might as well take the heart out of my body," he says to the wealthy man. "God gave her to me because you turned your back upon her." Cass replies, "I've repented of my conduct in that matter". Not long ago, a case very similar to this appeared in the news: a child's natural father wanted his son back after another family had adopted him. The court awarded the natural parents custody of the child in that case. Is it right for a natural father to claim a child after other people have raised it as their own? Do you think Godfrey's repentance gives him that right?

•Eppie turns down the Cass' offer of adoption on the principle that she wouldn't like having to get used to better things, and on the fear that the people who have loved her would find it impossible to relate to her any more if she were wealthy. Do you think she made the right choice? Do you agree with her? Do you think there might have been another solution to this problem?

•Consider Godfrey Cass's wives; Nancy Lammeter and Molly Farren. They are obviously *un*-like in some ways; one is a lower class drug addict, the other, the beautiful, favored daughter of a gentleman. Are they alike in any ways? Is there any quality both women have that might have drawn Godfrey to them. Which woman do you like better?

•Almost everyone dislikes something about *Silas Marner;* even George Eliot's staunchest defenders find that something in the novel makes them uncomfortable. Are there parts of the novel you dislike? Why?

About the Essayist:

Andrew J. Hoffman is the author of: *Inventing Mark Twain* a biography of Samuel Langhorne Clemens; *Beehive,* a novel; and *Twain's Heroes*, *Twain's Worlds.* A visiting scholar at Brown University, he holds a Ph.D. in Literature from Brown.